Jayne Clews

A catalogue record for this book is available from the British Library

Published by Ladybird Books Ltd
27 Wrights Lane London W8 5TZ
A Penguin Company

2 4 6 8 10 9 7 5 3 1

LADYBIRD and the device of a Ladybird are
trademarks of Ladybird Books Ltd

© Disney MM
102 Dalmatians based on the book The Hundred and One Dalmatians by Dodie Smith,
published by Heineman Ltd.

Ladybird

After three years in a prison hospital, Cruella de Vil was ready to be set free. Helped by the clever Doctor Pavlov, Cruella had learned to love dogs, and now she HATED furs!

Doctor Pavlov knew that only one thing could turn Cruella back to her old self – if she were to see a Dalmatian when Big Ben chimed.

The judge warned Cruella, "If you do go back to your old ways, then your entire fortune will go to the dogs in Westminster."

Then he let Cruella go.

That same day, Chloe Simon had some bad news. Her job, as a probation officer, was to make sure that people who had just come out of prison stayed out of trouble. And now she learned that she would have to look after Cruella de Vil! Chloe shivered when she thought of what Cruella had done not so long ago.

She couldn't believe that someone like Cruella could change – and neither could Dipstick, Chloe's Dalmatian. He had been one of the original 99 puppies stolen by Cruella. Now he was worried for his beloved Dottie and their own puppies, Little Dipper, Domino and Oddball.

On return to her mansion, Cruella ordered her servant Alonso to lock away all her old furs.

Then, as soon as she heard that a dogs' home in Westminster was about to be closed, she decided to rescue it. Kevin, the owner of the Second Chance Dog Shelter, couldn't believe his luck.

Kevin loved his dogs so much that he was willing to do anything to keep them – even if it meant trusting Cruella! In fact, he loved dogs so much that even his parrot, Waddlesworth, behaved like a dog and refused to fly!

Over the next weeks, Chloe kept a close eye on Cruella de Vil. She watched as Cruella transformed the Second Chance into a palace with luxurious couches and gourmet meals for the dogs. Cruella even gave the dogs new hairstyles and bubble baths!

But Chloe was suspicious of Cruella and
warned Kevin about her. Chloe liked
Kevin and soon they became good friends.

Chloe hated being away from her
Dalmatian family, so she often took them
with her to the office. Though she made
sure to hide them away in an upstairs
room, whenever Cruella de Vil came
to see her!

However, on one of these visits, Cruella caught sight of the puppies. She rushed to pet them – but just then Big Ben chimed…

At once, Cruella's hair sprouted wildly from her head, then she raced out into the street, shouting evilly, "Cruella's ba-a-a-ck! Hahahaha!"

Rushing inside her mansion, Cruella unlocked the door to her fur room.

"At last!" she gasped, wrapping furs around her. "At last!" Then she picked up her old design for a spotted Dalmatian coat, and smiled. *This time,* she decided, *she would need 102 Dalmatian puppies – she wanted a hooded coat!*

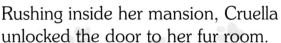

So first she sent out Alonso to start stealing Dalmatian puppies. Next, she contacted her old friend Jean-Pierre LePelt, the famous furrier, and told him to begin work. Then she thought up a plan for Kevin...

The next morning, at the Second Chance Dog Shelter, Kevin received an anonymous call about some abandoned puppies. When they arrived at the shelter, he was surprised to find that they were all Dalmatians!

Suddenly the police arrived, with an anonymous letter.

It said that Kevin had been stealing the Dalmatian puppies to make it look like Cruella was up to her old tricks again! And if Cruella went back in prison, then Kevin would be able to claim her whole fortune for the dogs of Westminster.

The police saw the Dalmatians in the shelter and believed the letter. Then they put Kevin and his animals into prison.

Everything was going exactly to Cruella's plan. Next she had to find a way to steal the three last puppies that she needed for her coat. And she knew exactly the ones she wanted.

That night Cruella held a dinner party for some friends and their dogs. She invited Chloe and Dipstick, and then told LePelt to steal Dipstick's puppies.

But when Cruella was busy with the meal, her own dog Fluffy showed Dipstick the way to the fur room, and Chloe followed them.

Chloe gasped in horror, when she saw the design for the Dalmatian puppy coat.

Suddenly Chloe heard an evil voice from behind. "Surprise!" sneered Cruella. Then Cruella locked Chloe in the fur room!

Luckily Dipstick escaped and arrived home just in time to leap into LePelt's truck where Dottie and their puppies had been locked away.

Soon all the dogs in London were barking the news – Oddball had managed to sound the alarm on the Twilight Bark, just before LePelt had dognapped her.

The news reached the animals in Kevin's cell – so Waddlesworth crept over to the guard, stole his keys, and set Kevin and the others free.

Meanwhile, with Fluffy's help, Chloe had managed to escape too. She arrived at her flat at the same time as Kevin. The place was deserted, but Kevin's dog Drooler found a clue – LePelt had dropped his railway ticket for the 10 o'clock Orient Express train.

Chloe and the pets raced across town.

At the station, Cruella was checking the puppies on the platform. Suddenly, she picked up Oddball. "A rat!" she shrieked, and dropped the puppy to the ground.

Oddball wasn't good enough for Cruella's coat – this little puppy had no spots! But Oddball wanted to be with her brothers. And as the train moved off, Oddball tried to jump onto it!

Just then Chloe and the others arrived.

"She'll be killed!" Chloe cried when she caught sight of Oddball.

For once in his life, Waddlesworth knew he had something to fly for. Madly flapping his wings, he scooped up Oddball, and dropped her safely onto the train.

"Follow those puppies!" said Chloe.

* * *

As the train pulled into Paris, Oddball and Waddlesworth watched LePelt unload the puppies into a van. Then he drove them to his workshop. As Oddball and Waddlesworth made a hole for the puppies to escape, Kevin and Chloe arrived to help – even Alonso joined in. He'd had enough of Cruella, LePelt and their evil ways.

Cruella was furious. She refused to let the puppies get away and tried to trap them in the bakery next door.

But Cruella was no match for 102 Dalmatians. In the end, she was baked into an iced cake and handed over to the police!

Several days later, Alonso arrived at the Second Chance Dog Shelter with a cheque. The judge had kept his promise – because Cruella had gone back to her old ways, all her money had gone to the dogs. The celebrations began – but that day no one was happier than Oddball. Her spots had finally arrived!